ESCAPADE JOHNSON
and
THE WITCHES OF BELKNAP COUNTY

written by
Michael Sullivan

illustrated by
Joy Kolitsky

PUBLISHINGWORKS, INC.
EXETER, NH
2008

PublishingWorks, Inc.

60 Winter Street

Exeter, NH 03833

603-778-9883

For Sales and Orders:

1-800-738-6603 or 603-772-7200

LCCN: 2008930877

ISBN: 1-933002-91-3

ISBN-13: 978-1-933002-91-0

$6.95

INTRODUCTION

Well, it's me, Escapade Johnson, again. I'm still sitting here in Sanbornton, New Hampshire, the most boring kid in the most boring town in the most boring state in the whole world. I still want to be a writer, but there *still* isn't anything exciting going on around me. So, for now, I'll just have to wait for my big chance.

In the meantime, I need to "hone my craft," as Mrs. Bartgauer says when she is talking about how all of us in the fifth grade at Sanbornton Elementary School have the ability to be great writers. I think she tells us this hoping it will inspire more than three of us to actually hand in a writing assignment. It generally doesn't work.

Anyway, honing my craft, according to Mrs. Bartgauer, means always writing, even when there isn't anything to write about. She talks about the difference between "message" and "voice," but it all seems to be the same to me, since I am *never* going to read anything I write out loud.

I still can't tell you about the time I accidentally set the only fire truck in Sanbornton on fire, because of something my mom calls the "statute of limitations," which in plain words means I have to keep my mouth shut for the next four and a half years. So today's writing for the sake of writing will be about the run-in some of us fifth graders had with the Witches of Belknap County, complete with lightning bolts from a clear sky, poisonous plants from New Guinea, malevolent vampire bats, and the mysterious grave of a teenage girl.

Enjoy.

CHAPTER 1

How do you know it's been an unusually cold and snowy winter in Sanbornton? Try this on for size: one Tuesday afternoon in early February, almost half of the fifth grade of Sanbornton Elementary School was in the Sanbornton Public Library. The other half would have been there as well, but they probably got lost trying to find the place. We are not the most studious class ever.

I was there to find a new book on mountain climbing, my current obsession since the entire fifth grade of Sanbornton Elementary School had climbed Mount Moosilauke on a field trip. All right, *most* of us climbed the mountain. Well, to be honest, only three of us actually climbed it, if you include Mrs. Bartgauer, our homeroom teacher. But half of us made it part of the way up the mountain and almost all of us at least made it off the bus in one piece. I love climbing, and I want to be a writer, so when I found out people actually climb mountains and write books about it . . . well, I was hooked.

Melinda Trackson was there, too, but the librarians *knew* her by name (can you believe it?), so I guess she was there a lot. She was hanging around the biology section studying up on her current obsession, which was actually our science teacher Mr. Hauteman. He was currently into duckbilled platypuses, and she wanted to know everything there was to know about them so she could always be the first to raise her hand in class. What a waste of time. She is always the only one to raise her hand in every class and have the correct answer. And in science class, Mr. Hautemen always calls on her, she is always right, Mr. Hauteman always smiles at her, and she always giggles. The whole thing is annoying.

Benny Black was reading a magazine called *The New Yorker* and mumbling about one-horse towns where you can't even get a decent soy mocha latte. He'd only been in New Hampshire for eight months, but it was already losing its small town charm for him.

Marjorie Jackson was trying to sit very still, her long arms and legs wrapped around her in impossible knots, looking warily at a spinning rack of paperbacks that she had already knocked over . . . twice. Marjorie is tall . . . in the way that NBA players and Davy Gilman's sandwiches are tall. She has never been anywhere but the back row in a class picture, and always in the center with the boys spread out right and left around her. And you didn't want to be the boy right next to her, or rather, right next to her elbows. Marjorie grew too fast, and she never could quite get her body under control. Arms and legs flying, she is a bloody nose looking for a place to happen.

Cherilyn Travis and Katrina Finink were huddled in a corner, giggling and fascinated, I guess, by something they had found in a couple of very brightly colored books. Davy Gilman and Jimmy Whitehorse were in another corner, grunting, belching, and staring at Cherilyn and Katrina. I remember when they used to make disgusting noises to scare girls away. Now they seemed to be trying to impress the girls with fake farts. Sad. I went back to watching Melinda.

"Let's try that one!" Katrina shouted suddenly, pointing to a page.

"We'll need a guinea pig," Cherilyn said, looking around. Davy and Jimmy seemed to disappear from where they had been watching the girls and then suddenly reappear, as if by magic, right in front of Cherilyn, who dissolved into a fit of giggles.

"What?" asked Davy, trying to look as uninterested as he could while leaning over to see what the two girls were reading.

"I guess you guys will do," laughed Katrina. "Give me your hand."

Davy recoiled, wrapping his arms together for protection, but Jimmy's hand was out in a flash. Katrina took it and spun it palm-up. Jimmy actually whimpered. All right, I'll admit, I was more than a little curious and slipped a few feet closer to watch.

Katrina and Cherilyn now bent over Jimmy's hand and studied it up close, their noses only inches away. They whispered a few words, rechecked his palm, and nodded in satisfaction.

"Oh, Melinda. Could you come over here for a sec?" Cherilyn called in a sing-song voice.

Melinda looked up from the books she was returning to the shelves and hesitated.

"Just come on over. We're doing a little experiment." Cherilyn looked over at Jimmy and added very slowly, "That's when you try something out."

I guess "experiment" was the magic word. Melinda can't resist anything that even sounds scientific. She shrugged and walked over to Katrina, who was still holding Jimmy's hand while he stood sighing softly. Without warning, Cherilyn snatched Melinda's hand, turned it palm-up, and pushed it up side by side with Jimmy's.

"What gives?" Melinda yelled, and tried to pull her hand back, but Cherilyn had it in a two-handed death grip. I knew what was going on, and couldn't help but wonder what Cherilyn would find in Jimmy's and Melinda's hands. I almost wished I'd volunteered to be the guinea pig.

Mrs. Limburger, one of the librarians, poked her head around a stack and called out, "Melinda,

Dear, is there anything wrong?"

"No, no," she called back, trying to look relaxed. Cherilyn and Katrina used the momentary distraction to lean over the two hands and study them intensely. Mrs. Limburger disappeared again, and suddenly the two girls looked disappointed.

"I don't see a love match here," Cherilyn said with exaggerated sadness. I realized then that I had been holding my breath, and let it out a little louder than I wanted to.

"Me neither," Katrina replied. "We need a different subject for comparison." She turned to Jimmy. "In this case, a subject isn't something you study in school, it is a person in one of those *ex-per-i-ments.*"

At this point, I felt a strange urge to get up

and move closer. I couldn't help but wonder what Cherilyn might find if she put my hand next to Melinda's.

Cherilyn looked right past me and called out, "Benny, can we see you for a minute?"

"No!" shouted Melinda, pulling her hand away.

"No!" shouted Jimmy even louder, and pulling his hand away even faster.

CHAPTER 2

Half an hour later, our whole group had pulled up chairs around one big table as Katrina and Cherilyn spread out the books they had been collecting.

"Wow, are these all books about witches?" asked Davy as he picked up one of them. From the way he held it, I think he was unsure which end he was supposed to open.

"The proper term is *Wiccans*," Cherilyn corrected, sounding just the way most teachers would make a point of *not* sounding. "Wicca is a very old religion practiced by people who are sometimes called witches."

Witches? Not a good topic to bring up, at least not around here; not in Belknap County, New Hampshire.

"But these books are full of spells, right?" Benny asked. "Do they tell you how to turn people into frogs? And how to turn other people into snakes? And how to tell the snake-people to eat the frog-people?"

"That is *not* what Wicca is all about," Cherilyn said icily. "Wicca is about healing and wholeness and love." Funny, I thought, Cherilyn looked exactly like she was about to turn Benny into a frog.

"Oh yeah, like you need black hats and broomsticks for that kind of stuff," Jimmy said laughing, then stopped dead when Katrina gave him a dirty look.

"Seriously," I said, "these Wiccans aren't real witches. Real witches cast spells and do evil magic and dance with demons, right?"

"No. Real witches honor peaceful goddesses and seek balance in the universe, and they are beautiful, not old and warty, and they wear crystals, not floppy black hats, and they can make handsome men fall in love with them and . . . "

Cherilyn looked up like she was waking from a dream and found the rest of us staring down at her like we were waiting for the nice men with the straitjackets to come and take her away.

"Well, at least they don't wear floppy black hats," she said, and started studying the page in front of her as if the secret to eternal youth and beauty was written there in very small print.

"Look out, they heard you!" hissed Jimmy, and he dove behind a low book stack as the library door opened and three old women shuffled in.

"Who heard?" asked Benny.

"The Witches of Belknap County," breathed Katrina and Cherilyn together, and they quickly started piling up the spell books and shoving them onto the nearest shelf. Melinda stifled a laugh, but no one else was laughing. All our eyes followed the three women. One of them was tall and gaunt and dressed all in gray, one of them was of middle height with raven-black hair that hung straight well past her waist, and one was short and plump and dressed in a glaring combination of reds and oranges.

They stopped just inside the doorway and bowed their heads together. Then with a flourish, they all spun on their heels. One turn, two turns, three, and away they spun in different directions. Davy, Jimmy, and Katrina dove under tables as the short, stout one hurried by on her tiny feet that poked out from the hem of her bright orange skirt. Cherilyn stood frozen, staring at the dark-haired one, who seemed to glide down an aisle, her head spinning smoothly as she kept her eyes locked on Cherilyn. I had the strange impression that her head had almost spun all the way around before she disappeared behind a large book stack.

Mrs. Limburger and Mrs. Colby, the two librarians, bustled around excitedly, pulling some of the library's oldest books off the shelves and chasing the three old women around, then returning those books and scrambling for others.

Benny stood perfectly still, watching all this with a baffled look.

"What is all this? Who are those women?"

Melinda grabbed him by his arm and sat down with him in a couple of chairs near me.

"They are three perfectly normal women who have gotten a terrible and undeserved . . . " she glared at the three classmates cowering under the tables " . . . reputation."

"Yeah," hissed Jimmy. "An undeserved reputation for turning children's fingers and toes black, for making cats bark and dogs meow, and for making it rain on important baseball games."

"Exactly!" said Melinda, then she looked suddenly confused. "Wait . . . "

"They are the Witches of Belknap County," Cherilyn said in a low voice between clenched teeth. "Miss Queril Taek, Miss Anne Thrope, and Miss Doris Meanor, the scariest of the bunch."

Miss Taek had the long hair and Miss Thrope was the short one. It's not like they weren't scary, but Miss Meanor was legendary. She was the tall and bony one, and the stories about her were passed on from class to class in Sanbornton Elementary. Seven Years ago, she was visiting the school, apparently to make the teachers even meaner, when a dozen fourth graders claimed that she looked at their lunch trays and all their milk turned sour. The aftermath was kind of gross, of course. But Miss Meanor had a reputation for staring at kids until they had to look in her eyes, then staring into their eyes until they ran away.

"They all live together in an old haunted house on Old Loggers Road," added Davy, stretching his head out from beneath the table to see if the coast was clear.

"That's where they do their evil spells," Jimmy hissed. "That's where they secretly turned Mrs. Lissard into a zombie. She's been the principal here for two hundred years!"

"Oh, listen to yourselves," Melinda exclaimed, exasperated. "For one thing, Sanbornton Elementary School is only fifty years old, so Mrs. Lissard couldn't have been principal for that long. And for another, what do you actually know about these three old ladies? For all you know, they're retired school teachers who spend all their time baking cookies."

"And that would mean they aren't witches?" Jimmy asked. "I would think 'witch' is a great retirement job for a teacher. They'd have plenty of practice."

"And I wouldn't eat any cookie one of them baked," stated Davy. Everybody looked at him wide-eyed. Actually, you had to open your eyes pretty wide just to see all of Davy at once.

"I didn't know there was anything you wouldn't eat," Benny replied with a look of genuine shock.

"I mean, what if they use the blood of their victims to make the batter?"

"Even so . . . " muttered Benny to himself, shaking his head and plopping limply back into his seat.

CHAPTER 3

The discussion of the Witches of Belknap County continued for a long time, with Benny in the middle, apparently agreed upon as judge and jury, Melinda on one side, and Cherilyn and everybody else on the other. Marjorie stayed out of the whole thing, and so did I, of course. I would have liked to jump in with Melinda, but I've heard some pretty creepy stories about the three old women who lived in an old, run-down house at the end of a dark dirt road. When pets disappeared, kids all over town blamed the witches for stealing them for their spells. I even heard my dad whisper to himself that the Witches of Belknap County were to blame when Laserdiscs went off the market and his store was stuck with five boxes of discs that they couldn't sell, which he still complains about it to this day.

Every kid within twenty miles is afraid of them. Even some adults, who remembered the three from when they were kids, pulled their children close when the trio walked past. Dogs bark whenever they walk by—and yes, dogs bark whenever I walk by—but that doesn't mean they're witches, does it?

"Really," I said, my voice even shakier than usual, "we don't have any *proof* that they are witches."

Cherilyn was the one who finally came up with a plan to settle the matter.

"Then let's get proof. Let's see what kind of books they take out. I bet it's all witch stuff."

Benny looked a little uncomfortable as he pointed to the pile of books Cherilyn and Katrina had shoved on a nearby shelf.

"But you're looking at witch books. Are *you* witches?" Benny asked, looking genuinely confused.

"These aren't books about real witches," Cherilyn snapped.

"But you said Wiccans were the real witches and the evil kind weren't real," Jimmy added with uncharacteristic logic.

"Would you like me to tell those three you were tormenting their black cat?" Cherilyn hissed at him. Jimmy went pale and shook his head so hard I think I heard something pop.

"All right," Cherilyn continued, satisfied that she had silenced all opposition. "Let's split up and follow each one of the witches to see what they're checking out."

Melinda jumped in. "Hey! It's not a fair test if you start off thinking that they're witches."

Cherilyn turned on her. "That's fine, we don't need you. Jimmy and Davy, you follow Miss Taek. Benny and Escapade, you follow Miss

Meanor. Katrina, Marjorie, and I will follow Miss Thrope."

"Why do we get the scariest one?" Benny objected.

"What makes you think *I* want anything to do with this?" was my objection.

"You're a part of this," Cherilyn said, poking me in the chest with her finger, "because you chicken out of everything. And you two get the scariest one because you don't believe they're witches anyways."

"I never said I didn't—" I began, but Melinda cut me off.

She turned on Benny and me and said, "I can't believe you two would *even* be a part of this. Those women don't need to be harassed by a bunch of juvenile monkeys with paranoid fantasies."

That, as well as Cherilyn's chicken comment, was enough to get me to agree. Cherilyn wasn't going to call me a chicken, and Melinda wasn't going to tell me what I could and couldn't do. Of course, looking back, I did let Melinda call me a monkey, and I did let Cherilyn tell me what to do, but at the time it seemed to make sense. Besides, Cherilyn was right. Deep down, I really didn't believe there were real witches, so how dangerous could three old ladies be?

"All right, I'm in."

"Great. Now, everybody, try to be discreet." Cherilyn turned towards Jimmy and whispered, "That means try not to be noticed." Then to all of us again, "If anyone gets caught and turned into a toad, you can live in my bathtub."

Davy's knees seemed to buckle at the thought. I knew exactly how he felt. Living in Cherilyn's bathtub . . . now that would almost be worth eating flies for the rest of your life.

Melinda stared at each of us in turn, rage and disbelief clouding her face. "I am not having anything to do with this lunacy!" she said before storming out of the library.

The rest of us all gave a nod and scattered throughout the library. Benny and I decided to split up and come upon Miss Meanor from opposite sides.

I buried my hands in my pockets and tried to whistle to sound casual. The sound echoed in the old library and came back to me sounding like one of those old songs my parents listen to. That was almost as creepy as the witches, so I stopped immediately. I sauntered around a huge book stack just in time to see Miss Meanor glaring down at Benny, who apparently didn't understand the meaning of the word "discreet."

"I say, young man, is there something I can do for you, or would you like to just hover around me like a bad smell for the next hour?"

Benny's lips trembled so much that speaking would probably have been impossible.

"In that case, I suggest you git!"

She raised the book she was holding like she was going to swing it at him and my heart froze. The book was old, dusty, and bound in leather. Cute little stories about big-hearted steam engines did not come in books that were old, dusty, and bound in leather. Benny turned and ran, and in one smooth motion, Miss Meanor spun on her heel and was staring directly into my face. Her eyes seemed to grow and expand until I could see nothing but two huge pupils blotting out everything else.

"I said *git!*" she cried, and I was gone—out the door, down the steps, and off into the snowy afternoon. I only caught a glimpse of Jimmy diving out of a library window, followed by half of Davy. The other half must have been stuck, but I wasn't about to stop and help him.

When Miss Meanor had raised the book above her head in front of Benny, I had gotten a perfect view of the title, and that title scared me more than the giant eyeballs of one of the Witches of Belknap County.

CHAPTER 4

"The Poisonous Plants of Papua New Guinea!"

The rest of the assembled fifth graders in the Sanbornton Elementary School cafeteria gasped in horror when they heard the title. Well, many of them did. Melinda was glaring angrily at me. Jimmy was staring, entranced, at Katrina in her long denim skirt. Davy was eating an egg salad sandwich, and while he may have tried to gasp, he ended up choking.

"That cinches it!" cried Cherilyn triumphantly.

"Why?" challenged Melinda. "What does that prove?"

"What would she want with poisonous plants if she wasn't making poison?"

"This is New Hampshire . . . in the dead of winter! I doubt she would find any of those plants from Papua New Guinea growing around here. Hey! Maybe she is making a traditional Papua New Guinean stew and doesn't want to use the wrong vegetables."

"That's ridiculous."

"And the rest of this isn't?"

Benny was looking doubtfully at the steamed vegetables on his plate.

"What's the matter?" I asked.

"You don't think this green stuff comes from Papua New Guinea, do you?"

Either Cherilyn couldn't answer this, or she just chose not to. Instead, she went on with her impromptu witch trial.

"Katrina and I saw Miss Thrope check out *Vampire Bats: the Mystery, the Majesty, the Malevolence*." When she saw the lost look on Jimmy's face, she said, "That means the evilness."

Jimmy looked half annoyed, half impressed.

Davy reported next. "Miss Taek took out this book covered with stars and moons and planets."

"See!" said Katrina, jumping up with excitement. "She's a Divinist ... Divinationer ... Divinisher ... she's a stargazer!"

Her sudden leap made an unwary fourth

grader stumble, almost dropping his tray of food. Marjorie dove to steady him, but ended up knocking over twelve third graders with a stray elbow. Fortunately, they all landed on a soft pile of second graders.

"Mr. Hauteman has books with stars and planets on them," Melinda said coldly, her jaw set and her teeth clenched, almost daring anyone to accuse *him* of witchcraft.

"But Mr. Hauteman doesn't live in a haunted house with seven thousand cats and two other witches!" Davy stated triumphantly, as if he had scored the final, unarguable point.

"They only have one cat," said Melinda flatly.

"How do you know?" Davy asked, suddenly looking very suspicious. "Been hanging out there casting spells? I knew nobody could get straight A's without supernatural help."

"I volunteer at the animal shelter, meat-for-brains. I was there when they got it, and they have to say what other pets are in the house when they adopt."

"I hear they call him 'West,'" added Marjorie helpfully. "That's a pretty weird name for a cat."

"They live in New England and have a cat called 'West'?" I said. "This is about as far north and east as you can get without falling into the Atlantic Ocean."

"That *is* a funny name for a cat," Katrina said, scrunching up her nose as if the name smelled rotten.

Melinda suddenly looked thoughtful. "It's

the fourth wind," she muttered, staring hard at nothing at all.

"Right, of course," Cherilyn said. "You need four witches to make a coven, one for each wind: north, south, east, and west. The cat is their fourth. I bet it isn't really a cat at all. It's probably their familiar, an enchanted witch in cat form."

"See, you do know way too much about this witch stuff!" Davy cried, pointing a shaky finger at Melinda.

Melinda sputtered for a second then pointed at Cherilyn. "She knows as much as I do about this and you don't call her a witch!"

"Witches don't wear pink," Davy stated flatly.

"Let's focus here, people!" Cherilyn didn't look happy to have the attention off her. "The important thing is that we know they have a witch cat."

"That's going a bit far, don't you think?" Melinda shook her head. "I just meant that's probably where it got its name. But yes, if they fancy themselves witches, they would like the idea of a foursome and would name their cat for one of the winds."

"That's it," pronounced Cherilyn, banging the table with one of Katrina's heeled shoes, which she was using as a gavel. "Miss Taek, Miss Meanor, and Miss Thrope are hereby found guilty of being the Witches of Belknap County. Now what shall we do about it?"

There was a stunned silence around the cafeteria table, while chaos reigned all around.

"What do you mean 'do'?" Davy asked tentatively.

"And what do you mean 'us'?" Marjorie added.

"Well, don't you think we ought to stop them?"

Everyone looked at Cherilyn as if she had suggested naked bullfighting.

"Stop them from doing what?" Benny asked.

"Isn't being a witch illegal?" Cherilyn asked, apparently shocked that her course of action would be questioned.

"It was," Davy said, "like a billion years ago."

"Yeah," snorted Melinda. "The dinosaurs invented fire so they could burn witches."

It looked like Davy couldn't decide whether to look confused or angry, so he tried to do both at once. I think he looked like how a monkey would look if it was trying to do multiplication tables in its head.

Marjorie asked, "Why? Why was being a witch against the law?"

"Because witches worshipped devils and goblins and, you know, evil things," Katrina hissed.

"And that's not illegal anymore?"

"Naw," replied Jimmy. "My uncle worships the devil and nobody bothers him."

"You're uncle, the part-time motorcycle mechanic with all the tattoos and body piercings?" Cherilyn sneered.

"No, that one's a Presbyterian. I'm talking about my uncle the high school principal. Nobody in my family talks to him much."

"Nobody cares about your stupid uncle!" Cherilyn interrupted. "This is much more important! If they are witches, then they're probably up to all kinds of evil deeds, like making livestock sick, and making rivers run red, and calling down giant frogs from the sky to eat the crops."

"I think you're mixing up your curses with your plagues," Benny pointed out. "Besides, nobody raises crops in Sanbornton anymore, or livestock, for that matter."

"You raise cockroaches," Marjorie pointed out. Everyone was quiet for a second, but decided not to go there.

"And Mrs. Chapman down the street from the school!" Jimmy added. "One of her chickens died just last week."

"You can't blame the witches for that, spaghetti-brain, it was hit by a car," Katrina hissed.

"Um, actually," I found myself saying, "Miss

Taek was driving the car. And I heard that the chicken tried to fly away and the car flew up in the air to hit it!"

"Chickens don't fly, Escapade," Marjorie Said.

"A car and a chicken both fly, and you think the problem is with the chicken?" Melinda shot right back at her.

But I wasn't done. "Do you think witches made animals sick by running them over in the past? What did they use before cars?"

Katrina looked confused. "Is it possible to drive evilly?"

"Well, they must be up to no good, and we should stop them," stated Cherilyn, once more grabbing the attention of the whole table.

"Should we call the police?" Marjorie suggested.

"They'd think we're nuts!" Benny cried.

"*I* think you're nuts," Melinda pointed out, but nobody seemed to notice.

"Benny's right. We need proof that there are crimes being committed. So who agrees with Benny's plan of sneaking into their house tonight and getting proof? I do!" Cherilyn threw her hand into the air.

Benny's mouth went slack. "But I didn't—"

"Me too," said Katrina, probably by reflex.

"Now wait a minute—" babbled Benny.

Davy and Jimmy raised their hands, probably not thinking beyond crawling around in the dark woods with Cherilyn and Katrina. "We're with Benny, too!" they chorused.

"I'm not!" cried Benny.

"I'm coming," Melinda stated flatly. All heads turned to stare at her in disbelief. "If I'm not there, you people will make up wild stories and nobody will be able to contradict them."

Slowly, the rest of the hands went up. I would rather have volunteered to sleep in the doghouse with Jimmy's vicious bulldogs, but when everyone else's hands went up, so did mine. I guess it's not easy to be only one not signing up, even for a dangerous mission to invade the lair of the Witches of Belknap County.

CHAPTER 5

The next night, the eight of us met at the end of Old Loggers Road, a glorified dirt path with a grass strip growing down the middle.

"Is Project Deception complete?" Cherilyn hissed.

"Project Whosiwazzit?" Jimmy asked.

Cherilyn placed her hands on her hips and glared at him. She was wearing a black hooded pullover jacket and a black knit hat, which would have helped hide her in the dark if her ski pants weren't so brightly pink that they glowed in the thin moonlight.

"Did everyone tell their parents they were going to a sleepover?" She pronounced the words so slowly and clearly that a squirrel might have understood her.

"Oh yeah," said Davy. "I told my folks I was sleeping over at Benny's house, Benny told his folks he was sleeping over at Jimmy's, Jimmy told his parents he was sleeping over at Escapade's, and Escapade told his folks he was sleeping over at my house."

Cherilyn gaped at him. "You were all supposed to be sleeping over at Jimmy's house. Nobody's parents would dare call over there to check."

"Yeah, nobody," Jimmy agreed laughing. He suddenly stopped and screwed up his face like he was trying to corner a particularly slippery thought. "Why not?"

"Do you remember the time my mom called your mom about a school bake sale and ended up calling 911 because of all the strange noises she heard in the background?"

"Hey! That was just a big misunderstanding, I mean, anything could make a donkey cry like that! And that was my uncle's parrot yelling, 'Stop or I'll shoot!' . . . oh, yeah, right."

"Anyway," Cherilyn continued with an exasperated sigh, "all the girls are supposedly at my house, and my folks are at a very fancy restaurant until late, so we have a couple of hours to get our evidence, go to the police, get our pictures taken for the newspaper, and get back before anyone notices we're gone."

"Won't they notice if we're in the newspaper? Won't they ground us for like twenty months, or even a year?" Benny asked warily.

"Well, by then we'll all be heroes, won't we? Nobody grounds heroes. Did Mr. and Mrs. Lindberg ground Charles for crossing the Atlantic without looking both ways? Did Mr. and Mrs. The Great ground Alexander for conquering the known world and not writing home? I doubt it. Geez, do I have to think of everything?"

I was about to argue, but couldn't decide where to begin.

"All right, we're all here and that's what matters. Benny, did you bring your camera?"

Benny proudly held up a 45-pound hunk of dials, lenses, and solid steel casement. His parents were into gadgets, and they did it right.

He pushed a button and a flash of light lit up the night for a hundred yards in every direction. Davy and Jimmy dove for cover behind some bushes like they had heard an explosion. Cherilyn, who had been staring directly into the flash, clawed at her eyes with pink-gloved hands.

"What are you trying to do?" screeched Katrina. "Call every witch from here to Stonehenge? Here we are! Come turn us all into gerbils!"

"Sorry," mumbled Benny, putting the camera away.

"All right, all right," Cherilyn stammered, blinking her eyes back into focus. "I think we should get going before somebody starts a bonfire."

"Me too," Katrina declared, and with that we all started up the road.

CHAPTER 6

Halfway up the road, Jimmy led us off into the woods so we could sneak up on the house from behind. The snow was so deep that he sank to his chest in two steps.

"Davy! A little help!"

Davy lumbered over, the snow just coming to halfway up his thighs. Jimmy grabbed the front of his coat and climbed up, hand over hand, scrambling with his feet for support, until he crawled over the dome of Davy's massive head. From there he perched on Davy's shoulders, waved his arm over his head, and shouted, "Forward!"

"Quiet," Cherilyn barked at him, then covered her mouth as she heard the word echoing through the woods.

"Oh, *this* is gonna work," Melinda mumbled, as we all trudged off through the snow.

It took us half an hour to scramble the hundred yards or so we could have covered in a few minutes if we had stuck to the road. The woods were so dark that Davy tripped over a root just as we reached the back yard of the house, sending Jimmy rolling into the open and burying Benny and Katrina below him in a huge snow bank. Davy rolled over and groaned, and Katrina came up sputtering.

"You ignorant, clumsy, moronic, ham-footed oaf! Jimmy get back here right now, you're going to be seen . . . " but she trailed off as she followed Jimmy's wide-eyed stare up to the roof of the house. There, on a flat part of the roof fenced in by a low railing, stood Miss Taek. Her long, flowing robes rippled in the wind while her arms were flung wide as she stood staring up at the sky. Suddenly there was a great gust of wind and the night exploded in a bright flash of light. Miss Taek was outlined against the open sky.

Katrina screamed, which was pretty good luck for me since nobody heard *me* scream. Nobody can compete with Katrina in a screaming contest.

Miss Taek turned to stare down from her great height.

A cat screeched.

Benny screeched.

"Run!" yelled Jimmy, scrambling to his feet and taking off blindly. When we saw where he was running to, we all ran after him.

He was heading straight for the back door of the house.

CHAPTER 7

Jimmy burst through the back door of the house, all seven of us close on his heels. Marjorie caught him by the arm just inside and spun him around.

"What are you doing?" she half screamed, half whispered.

"Got to get indoors ... away from witch ... witch see me ... evil eye ... " Jimmy was gasping for breath and shaking all over.

Cherilyn pushed through and ripped Jimmy's arm out of Marjorie's grasp. "But you ran into the witch's house, you idiot!"

"The witch's house . . . the witch's house . . . the *witch's* house?!"

"Did you see that?" Davy cried. "She called down lightning on a clear night."

"Yeah," said Benny. "And I got a great picture of it!"

"Picture?" asked Melinda, and she gave me a strange look. I couldn't believe Melinda was discussing photography at a time like this. But then . . .

"Wait a minute . . . " I said, as a thought started bouncing around my head like a pinball, but it was moving so fast I couldn't figure out what it was.

"Let's look around," Cherilyn whispered.

That drove away all other thoughts. Look around? Had she completely lost her mind? We all stared at Cherilyn in disbelief.

"Well, we're in here, aren't we? We might as well." And she started tiptoeing across the floor, looking right and left every few seconds and crouching as if she were slipping below some searching spotlight. She was cat-like, like some super sleuth in one of those Hollywood robbery movies that my dad is always showing on the monitors of his video store because he likes to imagine he could act in one.

Of course, each time her wet sneaker came down it made a loud squeak. I'm pretty sure a real super sleuth wouldn't make a noise that said, "Here I am!" every time she took a step. For the first time, I noticed we were in a kitchen, and we were dripping huge puddles of melted snow onto the linoleum floor.

The room was dark, but there was a slight glow of moonlight coming through the windows. Cherilyn was headed for a hallway, and Katrina, of course, was right behind her. Davy and Jimmy were not far behind. Marjorie, Melinda, Benny, and I looked at each other.

"Benny," said Melinda, "Did you take your picture before or after the lightning hit?"

"At exactly the same time," Benny said proudly.

"So the light from your flash . . . "

"Must have been swallowed up in the lightning flash."

Now that bouncing thought settled in my

brain. Marjorie, too, seemed to have grasped what happened. Benny, however, still didn't have a clue.

Suddenly, we heard a strangled cry from Katrina and we all spun toward the hallway. Of course, all we could see was complete darkness. So we hurried out of the kitchen and bumped into something huge and solid just through the doorway.

"There's a padded wall here!" Benny cried. "Is this some kind of insane asylum?"

"Stop poking my butt!" Davy yelled.

"Your butt," Cherilyn screamed, "Would take three javelins and a nuclear missile to properly poke, NOW MOVE IT or I'll poke you with my boot!"

"Watch it Pinky, or I swear I'll . . . "

"Sit on her?" Benny suggested.

". . . and flatten her like a pancake?" Benny added.

" . . . or stomp on her like a bug?" Benny corrected.

"Ouch!" Benny concluded, when Davy stomped on his foot.

"Double ouch!" Benny moaned, as Cherilyn stomped on his other foot."

"There's something . . . furry there," Katrina whimpered.

"Benny, take a picture," Melinda ordered.

"Of what?"

"It doesn't matter, just take one."

Benny pointed the camera and clicked. Of course, he pointed it right at Melinda, whose hands flew to her face at the bright flash. She was blinded, but the rest of us saw a brief glimpse of a huge wolf, fangs bared and fur bristling, just behind Katrina.

Cherilyn screamed out loud. Benny swung toward her at the sound and hit the shutter button again. Another flash, and an eagle appeared for a split second, wings spread, talons reaching for Davy's head. This time Benny screamed.

Everyone broke into different directions, banging into obstacles in the tight hallway and bouncing back into each other. Every time Benny struck something, he squeezed off another picture until the whole world seemed to be stuck in the frozen scenes of a strobe light. Bears reared and pawed the air. A huge snake was caught in mid-spring. Miss Thrope appeared, half the height and twice the width of the bear, and looking three times as fierce.

It's an army, I thought; an army of wild creatures Miss Thrope had enchanted to do her bidding.

"She's gonna turn us all into animals!" Marjorie wailed.

"We're all gonna be panther chow first!" Jimmy yelled, and we all ran through the first door we saw.

Suddenly the floor disappeared and we all plunged down a steep stairway, rolling and bouncing, and finally falling in a heap. Luckily, Davy was the first through the door, and we all landed softly on him. If he had been last . . . well, I don't want to think about that.

I'd seen enough horror films at my dad's store; I knew what would happen next. The walls would close in, the ceiling would come down on us, and we would be crushed almost as flat as if Davy really had fallen on us.

"Snake pit!" Cherilyn screeched. "I've been bitten by a slimy, disgusting snake!"

"Don't worry," Benny shouted triumphantly, wiping his mouth with the back of his hand. "I bit him back! And he wasn't that slimy." Cherilyn slapped him across the face, or at least tried to.

Legs and arms flailing, we started to untangle ourselves when suddenly all our eyes were drawn to a few flickering lights in the darkness. Across the basement from us, fires burned low over dark containers from which seeped strange, smoky vapors.

"Why, those are . . . " Melinda started.

" . . . Potions!" Jimmy cried. "It's an evil

witches' dungeon!" He started swimming through the mass of bodies, back up the stairs.

Suddenly, the lights were cut by a dark figure that seemed to rise up between us and the flames. The glow now outlined the figure of Miss Meanor. There was a loud pop, and a puff of brilliant green smoke shot into the air behind her. Now everyone began clawing their way back up the staircase and away from that stern, silent figure.

Jimmy hit the top of the stairs first and stopped dead in his tracks. There loomed the figure of Miss Thrope, filling the width of the doorway, and Miss Taek hovering above her. We turned, but Miss Meanor was perched at the bottom of the stairs behind us, blocking our escape. We were trapped.

CHAPTER 8

"**P**lease don't eat us!" Davy begged, choosing to fall on his knees before Miss Taek, tears running down his face.

"Or make us ugly like you!" Katrina pleaded.

"Shut up!" Marjorie snapped. "That isn't helping!"

"We won't tell anyone what you are, just don't turn us into anything . . . uh . . . scaly," Benny whimpered, falling to his knees.

Miss Taek's sharp voice silenced everyone else. "I couldn't eat you in a week," she sneered, staring down at Davy.

"And you shouldn't be talking about ugly with a make-up job like that!" Miss Meanor snapped at Katrina.

"And the Bolivian Scum Lizard may be scaly, but I suspect it has more brains than you do, young man," Miss Thrope spit at Benny. "Now will someone please explain what in the name of Lineas you are doing here?"

"Who's Lineas?" Jimmy asked, suddenly calmed by the riddle.

"He must be a great and terrible wizard," Cherilyn hissed.

"He's a scientist, and you are all a bunch of dodo birds," Melinda stated flatly and pushed her way through us to stand before Miss Thrope.

"Miss Thrope, let me apologize. This is all a big misunderstanding."

"Yeah!" Davy cried. "Eat her instead."

Melinda turned on Davy with a look so terrifying that he chose to cozy up a little closer to Miss Meanor, who put a cold, bony hand on his shoulder, prompting a few whimpers.

Melinda turned back to Miss Thrope. With a brashness that I will always admire, she said flatly, "These morons think that you are all witches."

With a calmness that will always chill my blood, Miss Thrope answered, "Oh yes, that whole 'Witches of Belknap County' nonsense again."

"Nonsense, huh?" cried Cherilyn, pushing past Melinda and pointing down to the flickering flames in the basement. "Do you call those bubbling caldrons nonsense?"

"Caldronsssss?" hissed Miss Meanor from the bottom step. "Young lady, do you even know what that word means?"

"It means a round-bottomed pot, usually made of iron!" piped in Jimmy, looking at Cherilyn with an air of triumph. This coming from the guy who had been knocked out of the Sanbornton Elementary School Spelling Bee in the first round three years in a row on the words "lake," "chair," and, oddly enough, "iron." Katrina huffed and looked ready to tell Jimmy how stupid he was when Miss Meanor cut her off.

"Exactlllllly." And with that, Miss Meanor threw a switch and the basement lit up like midday.

Three long tables were revealed in the middle

of the room, surrounded by metal cabinets and bookcases packed with big, modern textbooks. The tables themselves were made of very modern looking stainless steel, and the fires burned not under iron pots, but glass vials and beakers.

All right, I thought. Out of the classic movie *The Blair Witch Project* and into *Frankenstein*. At this point, I started to wonder if I spent way too much time watching videos at my dad's store. But that thought was quickly replaced by a feeling of raw terror, which, given the circumstances, was more normal of a response than running through old movies in my head. I could now wait to be eaten by a giant bug or crushed by an evil robot.

Melinda, though, gave a little squeak of glee and pushed past everyone to the first table. She stared in wonder at the bubbling green liquid, then down at an open book the size of three history textbooks.

"It's an electrolyte experiment!" she laughed, then turned to Miss Meanor. "How do you keep the ionization going? Are you using a special catalyst?"

Miss Meanor's face brightened into an excited smile, not a comforting sight by the way as she looked like a cannibal about to eat a five course (or five missionary) dinner, but she seemed to have forgotten everyone else and launched into a rapid discussion with Melinda apparently in some language I've never heard before. "It's a chloride mixture, but I am having trouble keeping the salt byproducts from contaminating the results. Have you any idea how to isolate them?"

"Do you have a centrifuge?"

"Yes, I thought of that, but the chloride crystals are so heavy they get separated out too, and the reaction bogs down."

"How about suspending ionized potassium in the . . . "

While the two of them rambled on in dictionary-speak, the rest of us decided we'd rather face Miss Thrope than listen to what was quickly starting to sound like science class. "Death before school," as Jimmy always says. Katrina went on the offensive.

"All right, those may not be potions, but what about all the wild, man-eating beasts you keep upstairs? Do you expect us to believe those are harmless pets?"

"Pets? No. Harmless? Well, judge for yourselves." And with that, Miss Thrope turned and climbed the last few steps back to the first floor. The seven of us now hung on the steps between two terrors: slavering beasts above, and an advanced science class with Melinda and Miss Meanor below. We all went up.

CHAPTER 9

We crowded around the doorway between the basement stairs and the dark hallway. Actually, most of us were crowded behind Davy, peering around him into the gloom. There were small glistening specks of yellow light, as if eyes were looking back at us out of the dark room, but that was all we could see. Suddenly, a spotlight lit up a corner of the room, and bared teeth leapt at us from the darkness.

Katrina, who had been pushed in front of Davy as we came up behind her, screeched and dove back for the stairs, bounced off Davy, and sprawled backwards into the paws of an enormous lion.

Katrina screamed again and scrambled away, wrapping her arms around the legs of a gigantic brown bear, reared up on his hind legs and pawing the air. Realizing her mistake, Katrina crawled away until she bumped her head into the shell of a sea turtle the size of a small car and fell back on her bottom, momentarily stunned.

Katrina's terrified screams died down and were replaced by Miss Thrope's shrill, hysterical laugh. One by one, more spotlights flickered to life, revealing a long hallway filled with creatures great and small, each frozen in their own individual beams of light. Miss Thrope was cackling away, her hand on a long line of light switches. I froze, trying to remember if it was bears or dinosaurs that could only see you when you moved. I was getting my outdoor survival movies mixed up with the dinosaur ones, and just when I could prove my mother wrong for all the times she told me watching videos was a waste of time.

But it wasn't just me. Nobody moved. More importantly, nothing moved.

"Stuffed," snorted Benny, running his hands along the Lion's back, and all of us released a breath.

"Specimens," Miss Thrope said, correcting him. "Biological specimens collected over many years and used in my biology classes when I was a professor at the University of New Hampshire. She glared down at Katrina, who was still sobbing quietly, her arms wrapped protectively around her knees.

Benny wasn't convinced. "But what about

Miss Taek's gazing at the stars and calling down lightning?!"

Miss Taek's high, cheerful voice jumped from her throat. "Gazing at stars, yes, but what's this about lightning?"

"You raised your hands and—"

A dazzling flash of light exploded in the room. Davy and Jimmy hit the floor.

"Yeah, that!" Benny cried.

I cleared my throat.

Benny looked at me, then down at my finger, which was hovering over the shutter button of the camera he was still holding. I had figured it out, well, after Melinda had given me a few hints, and when I wanted the flash of lightening I just reached over and pressed the button on his enormous camera. The electronic flash had done the rest.

"Oh," was all he could say.

Miss Taek's laughter seemed to clear away all fear in the room. "So *that* was the light that blocked out the brilliant setting of Mars! I must admit, I thought for a second some enchantment was afoot myself, a bright light like that on an otherwise clear night. But I bet there is some of the night's show left to be seen. Who wants to look through my telescope?"

"Telescope?" Marjorie echoed. "You have a telescope?"

"Well of course, Dear. What astronomer would be without a telescope?"

"An astronomer?" cut in Cherilyn. "You can tell the future by looking at the stars?"

"No, Dear, and let me fix your hair." She began to fuss with Cherilyn's hair, half of which was matted down with sweat, half of which was standing up with fright, and half of which was frizzed out from hat-head. I know that sounds odd, but Cherilyn has a lot of hair. Strangely, having her hair fixed seemed to calm Cherilyn a lot, like petting a cat, I guess.

"Astrologers tell the future by looking at stars. I'm an astronomer, a professor of astronomy, actually, retired. I am a scientist who studies the motion of stars and other things in the sky."

"I knew that," pouted Cherilyn.

"I did too," asserted Katrina as she scrambled back to her feet. And with that, seven fifth graders from Sanbornton Elementary school climbed a ladder through the roof of the little house to stare at Mars through Miss Taek's telescope.

An hour later, Miss Doris Meanor and Melinda had finished their chemistry discussion. (It turns out that Miss Meanor had been a professor at the University of New Hampshire as well. That'swhere the three had met.) Davy had finished hearing from Miss Anne Thrope about the eating habits of large, hairy mammals, and everyone else had stared through Miss Queril Taek's telescope until the cold drove us back inside. We then all sat around the table in the kitchen of the little house, eight fifth graders from Sanbornton Elementary School and the three Witches of Belknap County, sipping hot cocoa and soaking up the warmth.

"We must seem pretty silly thinking that all this witchcraft stuff is real," Marjorie laughed, wiping off the whipped cream she had somehow managed to get on her nose and eyebrows.

Miss Meanor's face went hard, and she looked long into Marjorie's eyes. Marjorie tried to meet the older woman's gaze, but in just a few seconds she had to lower her eyes. Still, Miss Meanor stared on, seeming now to be focused on a spot behind Marjorie, or in a different world altogether. Then, in an instant, she seemed to come to a firm decision. She pressed her bony hands to the table and pushed her long frame up to its full height.

"Anyone who is still curious about witchcraft, come with me."

She spun on her heels, grabbing a coat and hat from a peg on the wall, and walked out the back door without even looking to see if any of us followed.

Of course, we all did.

CHAPTER 10

Miss Meanor led us out through the back door of the house and onto a trail leading into the woods. There was fresh snow on the ground, but it was clear that she followed a well-worn path. The woods looked wild and untouched. If it weren't for the path, it would have been easy to believe that no human had been there in thousands of years. It was easy enough to imagine other creatures stalking those woods. Everyone else seemed to be thinking the same thing, and we all huddled together behind Miss Meanor. She may have been plenty scary, but not as scary as the woods at night.

Suddenly, the trees cleared and a wide glen sat before us. In the center of the clearing stood a cemetery next to a tiny, old stone church. The church was overgrown with vines, and the gravestones were buried in an avalanche of green moss and pure white snow. Miss Meanor walked between dozens of such markers as if they were no more than rocks in a field. Then she stopped in front of an ordinary looking marble gravestone. She stared blankly at the words etched on it, and we crept up around her to read too.

The stone simply read, "Josie Flagg, died 1761, age 19 years."

In a voice that seemed both sad and menacing, Miss Meanor began to speak.

"You all seem to have some crazy ideas about witchcraft and witches. I can't begin to guess where you get those notions, but if you want the real story, just listen to me."

Just then, a wind seemed to rise up from the ground beneath her, and her coat billowed out like the wings of some enormous bat. In the midst of that shadow, the moon reflecting off her eyes shone with an almost unnatural light. Tall as she was, Miss Meanor seemed to grow into a dark thundercloud that hung above us. When she spoke again, her voice was far away, echoing like it came from hundreds of years ago.

"Josie Flagg was born on an unusually cold evening in October, on the third anniversary of her parents' marriage. Doctors were few and far between in those days, so a midwife presided over the birth of the pretty baby girl. But the birth did not go well, and the mother became weaker and weaker, even after the child was born. John Flagg, the father, in fear and anguish begged the old woman to save his wife. She tried with all her arts, but, as happened too often in those days, the mother did not survive."

Katrina burst out in a little cry and clung to the first arm she could reach. It turned out to be Jimmy's arm, and she squeaked again, then clung to Cherilyn instead.

Miss Meanor glared at Katrina, then continued. "The husband was so full of grief that he denounced the old woman as a witch, even though he had no true reason to do so. Such was the suspicion of those times, so the people of the town believed him, and, not waiting for any court, they seized the woman and tied her to a stake in the town center."

I knew what that meant, but somehow listening to Mr. Oletome, our history teacher, talk about burning accused witches in a bright, warm classroom wasn't the same as listening to a six-foot tall, bony old woman talk about it in a snowy graveyard in the middle of the night.

"Just before they lit the fire, the old woman caught sight of John at the front of the crowd, and, knowing him to be her accuser, lowly whispered to him.

"'You say I am a witch, though I give you no cause. Well, if indeed I am a witch, be wary. That child is doomed to suffer the fate of her mother, for so closely are they tied. She too will die three years after she is wed—not a day sooner, not a day later.'

"With her prophecy spoken, the flames took her, one of the last accused witches known to have been killed in that sad chapter of the history of the American colonies."

"Nooooo," Jimmy breathed. "Really? A flame-broiled witch?" Cherilyn reached around Katrina's shoulder and slapped him on the back of the head.

"The father was beside himself with grief, and the words struck him to the core He devoted himself to the care of his daughter, raising her to be a kind and caring young woman. But always he kept her a strict distance from young men, always afraid of the old woman's prediction. When the girl was sixteen, though, he found out that she was secretly being courted by a farmer's son and that the two were in love. Immediately, he told her he was sending her away to live with relatives in Boston, and the next day she was put on a stagecoach and sent south.

"The young man, named Nathaniel, disappeared some days later, and many in town who suspected that there was something between Nathaniel and Josie began to whisper that he had gone off in search of his love. Josie believed this, too, and she waited for Nathaniel to come find her. But as weeks, months, and even years passed without word of Nathaniel, the girl had to admit that he had probably changed his mind."

"That's so sad," Marjorie moaned.

"If only that was the sad part," Miss Meanor shook her head. "Should I stop now? Should we all go back for more hot cocoa?"

"Yes!" screamed every brain cell in my head. But my mouth yelled, "No!" along with everyone else's.

"All right," Miss Meanor whispered, shaking her head. "Your choice. Josie returned to Sanbornton to take care of her father when his health began to fail. Now a young woman of nineteen, she suddenly found herself with more freedom than she had ever enjoyed, and she began to spend time with newfound friends who were more daring and adventurous than the people she had known. On a night out with them, talk turned to spooks and superstitions. Josie said she didn't believe in such things, and someone dared her to go and stand on a grave, as corpses back then were believed to reach out in the dead of night and pull the living down into the earth to share their graves. Josie accepted the challenge, but as no one would dare go as witness, Josie took along a pearl-handled knife to stick in the ground to mark where she stood.

"Josie strode confidently to the graveyard and stood before a wooden marker for a long while before plunging the knife into the ground. Then she stood and admired the stars shining brightly on a moonless night. No hand grabbed at her legs, and she laughed at the gullible fools who believed in such superstitions. But when she turned to leave, she felt a tug at her dress. A twig perhaps, she thought. She pulled harder, but the dress dragged back against her. She began to panic. She struggled to drag herself off the grave, but she was held fast. In desperation, she tried to leap away, but she fell in a heap, hitting her head on a nearby gravestone. The last thing she felt was something cold and hard biting deep into her foot.

"The next morning, the cries of the minister brought the townspeople to the graveyard. John Flagg heard whispers and pushed through the crowd, only to fall on his knees before the lifeless body of his daughter. A huge pool of blood spread out from the knife that she had thrust in the ground, pinning the hem of her skirt, eventually cutting deeply into her ankle as she kicked to get away.

"The minister, shaking uncontrollably, pointed

to the stone and said, 'John, look, the grave.'

"John saw the writing on the marker and began to howl anew with grief, but the towns people were confused. The name meant nothing to any of them, which was strange enough in a town as small as Sanbornton.

"'It's a sign!' cried the minister. 'Tell them. Tell them, John, or I will.'

"John lowered his head, his voice pained and hoarse. 'The boy in this grave is none other than the boy Nathaniel who once loved my Josie. I killed him nearly three years ago to keep him from marrying my daughter because a seeing woman told me she would die three years after she married. I scarred his face beyond recognition, then convinced the minister to help me bury him by saying that he was a drifter who had stumbled into my mill and that I wanted no trouble after the accident. But now I see that I blackened my soul for no reason, for the witch betrayed me, and here lies my daughter, both unmarried and dead.'

"'So,' said the minister, troubled by the confession, 'your evil deeds repay you, for now I am released of a vow I took three years ago this night. If you had confided in me, much sorrow could have been avoided, for she and the boy came to me and were secretly married, and they swore me never to tell a living soul about it for as long as either should live. That was three years ago this very night, the night you sent your daughter away.'

"The townspeople were so angered and frightened that they cast the minister out of their town and hung John Flagg from a tree that grew near the graveyard. You will find no stone to mark *his* grave. Men guilty of such crimes in those days were denied a Christian burial.

"For many generations afterwards, the boys and girls of Sanbornton would bring their sweethearts to stand on Josie's grave and pledge their love as a reminder that such pledges are forever, even unto death."

CHAPTER 11

Miss Meanor's voice trailed away until the last few words were barely audible. Then, in a voice much less far away, she said to us, "John Flagg was my great, great, great, great, great, great, great, great granduncle."

Cherilyn was clearly impressed. "So your great, great, great, great, great, great, great, grandcousin was cursed by a real witch? But that's just too cool!"

"Why thank you, Dear," she said, scowling at Cherilyn. "Yes, I'm very proud."

"Oh, but there's no talking to Miss Thrope on the subject of witchcraft. Her great, great, great, great, great, great, great grandmother was hanged as a witch at Salem."

"For real?" Katrina gasped.

"Oh yes, and Miss Taek's great, great, great, great, great, great, great granduncle was involved in the funniest case of mistaken identity ever in the history of witch trials. Imagine, they actually found a real witch, convicted him, then someone made a clerical error and they ended up condemning the wrong man."

There was a pause, as each of our mouths went dry. It was Jimmy who seemed to find enough moisture in his mouth to speak. "You mean they executed Miss Taek's great, great, great, great, great, great, great granduncle because they thought he was the real witch."

"Oh no," Miss Meanor laughed. "Don't worry your heads, children. They didn't hang him, they hung his best friend instead."

We all breathed easier.

Then Miss Meanor's face seemed to grow dark and her voice became low and husky.

"But they should have!"

And so our adventure with the Witches of Belknap County had a happy ending. Even better, I caught a cold tramping around the woods on a winter night, so I get to skip school and sit here exercising my "voice," as Mrs. Bartgauer likes to say, on the computer in my room.

I think Melinda and Miss Meanor may become great buddies. They agreed to meet every afternoon after school until Miss Meanor completes her new sports drink. It's hard to imagine that is what they were talking about over all those bubbling beakers, using all those big chemical terms. Yuck! I'll never drink Gatorade again.

Jimmy asked Miss Thrope if she would stuff his bulldog when he died and make him part of her collection. She was thrilled, and that started the strangest friendship I've ever seen. Marjorie and Miss Taek, too, have become fast friends, and Miss Taek says that if Marjorie grows any taller, she won't need a telescope to see the stars. She'll be close enough to see them with the naked eye.

Cherilyn and Katrina are back to their Wiccan love spells and are trying to get their hair to grow longer and shinier. Benny has been grumbling about "superstitious hicks," and claiming he never believed any of that witch nonsense.

Oh, and Benny won fifty dollars in the Belknap County Gazette photo contest for his picture of Katrina being startled by an enormous bear that looked like it was about to pounce. It was just one of Miss Thrope's stuffed displays, but it beat out the picture I took last summer of our town's only police cruiser floating down Sanbornton Creek, which was probably for the best. If Chief Porcine knew I was close enough to take that picture, I might have to answer some tough questions.

All in all, I think things settled down pretty quickly, which is the real curse of this dull little town. Even when something does happen, it doesn't last for long. Why, the time I accidentally released four dozen eels into the town's water tank, most of the town stopped yelling at me within a couple of weeks, and the Chinese restaurant in Laconia didn't even press charges, but that's another story for another day. I just need to stick my head out of the window now and hope my cold gets worse so I can stay home tomorrow and write. Till then, goodbye from Sanbornton, New Hampshire, home of the Witches of Belknap County!

About the Author

Michael Sullivan is a storyteller, juggler, chess instructor, librarian, and former school teacher who grew up in small town New Hampshire, and now lives in Portsmouth, NH. He has worked with kids in many settings, from summer camps to the Boston Museum of Science, and is rumored to have once been a kid himself. He is the author of the book *Connecting Boys With Books*, and speaks across the country on the topic of boys and reading. In 1998, he was chosen New Hampshire Librarian of the Year.

Visit Michael's website at:
http://www.talestoldtall.com/BoyMeetsBook.html